ONLY A MATTER OF TIME

A STORY FROM KOSOVO

D1489914

Look for other titles in the Survivors series:

SURVIVORS

ONLY A MATTER OF TIME

A STORY FROM KOSOVO

STEWART ROSS

BARRON'S

This book is gratefully dedicated to Jacqui Pick and the
students of the Croydon Writing Summer School for Able and
Talented Pupils: Nielson Olavo-Ganboa, Aaron Price, Helen
Lewarne, Jade Brown, Thomas Mullaney, Ellie Ross, André
Minott, Lee Millward, Amanda Rhamanohar, Danielle Paul,
Hannah Doe, Olivia Thornton, Tatiana Gree, Danielle Willis,
Claire Blott, Antonio Jewell, and Coretta Mills.

First edition for the United States, its territories and dependencies,
the Philippine Republic, and Canada published in 2002
by Barron's Educational Series, Inc.

Text © copyright 2001 by Stewart Ross
First published in Great Britain in 2001 by Hodder Wayland, an imprint of
Hodder Children's Books Limited.

The right of Stewart Ross to be identified as the author of this work has been
asserted by him in accordance with the Copyright, Designs, and Patent
Act of 1988.

Illustrations © copyright 2002 by Barron's Educational Series, Inc.

All inquiries should be addressed to:
Barron's Educational Series, Inc.
250 Wireless Boulevard
Hauppauge, NY 11788
http://www.barronseduc.com

Library of Congress Catalog Card No.: 2001097535

International Standard Book No.: 0-7641-5524-5 (Hardcover)
0-7641-2201-0 (Softcover)

Printed in Hong Kong
9 8 7 6 5 4 3 2 1

The publisher would like to advise readers that this book may
contain language and/or descriptions of events that some readers may find
disturbing. The purpose of this book is to give the reader a sense of what
life was like in Kosovo, from the perspective of people who lived there
during this time. The publisher does not necessarily endorse the views
expressed in this book.

Introduction

Kosovo is a province of Serbia, one of the largest states in the Balkans. Most Kosovans are Muslims of Albanian descent. The Serbs are largely Orthodox Christians. By the 1990s, the majority of Albanian Kosovans wanted their province to be an independent country. The Kosovo Liberation Army (the KLA) was formed to wage guerrilla war against the Serbs. Ibrahim Rugova, leader of the moderate Kosovo Albanians, hoped to win independence by negotiation.

For religious and historical reasons, the Serbs were deeply attached to Kosovo, although not many actually lived there. In 1998, the Serb leader, Slobodan Milosevic, began "ethnic cleansing" in Kosovo – forcing Kosovo Albanians to leave. Gangs of Serb thugs joined in the racist attacks, often with extreme brutality.

By the fall of 1998, the international community had decided that the bloody conflict in Kosovo had to stop. The Western alliance, NATO, threatened Serbia with air strikes if the ethnic cleansing did not stop. An uneasy cease-fire was agreed on. It did not resolve the problem and by the end of the year the fighting flared up once again.

When talks failed, in March 1999, NATO launched air strikes against the Serbs. In response, the Serbs stepped up their ethnic cleansing and hundreds of thousands of Kosovo Albanians fled abroad. In June 1999, Milosevic agreed to withdraw his forces from Kosovo and NATO troops moved in to restore law and order.

Only a Matter of Time is based on the Human Rights Watch report of the ethnic cleansing and murders that took place in a Kosovo village near the town of Pec in May 1999. The population was largely Albanian, although a handful of Serb families also lived there. Before the brutalities, relations between the two racial groups were amicable. To protect individuals still living in Kosovo, both Albanian and Serb, all names have been changed.

This map shows the area of Kosovo in which
Only a Matter of Time is set.

One

Beyond the Crossroad

The bus splashed to a halt halfway between the tire factory and the tractor service station.

"Toskik village!" called out Bujar, reaching forward to take a cigarette from the crumpled pack on the dashboard. "Anyone for Toskik?"

I didn't need to reply. Every day old Bujar stopped his battered bus at exactly the same spot and asked without thinking if anyone was getting off. And every day he made the same remark: "Oh! It's you, Miss Drita! So this is where you live, is it?"

Picking up my schoolbag, I clattered down the metal steps and out into the cold afternoon air. The door hissed shut behind me. As Bujar urged his bus off down the Pristina road, I heaved my bag onto my shoulders and began the steep climb up the road toward our village.

* * *

Father's blue Mercedes was parked on the road outside our house. Why isn't he at work? I wondered, opening the front door and dumping my bag on the floor.

Mother's voice called from the living room, "Is that you, Drita? Come and join us, please." She spoke in her do-as-you-are-told voice, which usually meant trouble. I sighed. What had I done wrong this time? I hoped they hadn't found out about Zoran.

The whole family was there. Fatime, Rukie, and Naser were squashed into an armchair watching TV. Mother, Father, and my elder brother Muhamet were sitting around the table. Although it was starting to get dark, no one had switched on the lights.

This looks grim, I thought. I prepared myself for a major scolding.

It did not come. Mother told me to sit down and listen to Father.

"It's bad news . . ." he began, frowning so hard that his caterpillar eyebrows met in the middle of his forehead. The cease-fire between the Serbs and the Kosovo Liberation Army had broken down completely. He had just heard of a terrible massacre near Racak, where forty-five Kosovo Albanians, our own people, had been brutally killed.

I did not ask him how he knew, just as I did not ask him where he got his money from. A man who ran a car repair business from a Pec backstreet should not be able to drive a Mercedes. Nor should he be able to afford the fees of my private school, the only Albanian school that was still open, nor sneakers costing seventy American dollars for his children, nor three color TVs. But Mr. Sadik Binaku, my father, did. There was a part of my father's life I didn't understand. Afraid of what I might learn, I loved him too much to ask.

"But it doesn't mean trouble around here, does it?" I asked.

"Here and everywhere, until we're free," muttered Muhamet. "Remember Halil?"

I looked at him and nodded. Halil Nebihu, a KLA member from the neighboring village of Pavlan, had been shot dead by the Serb police one night last November. They said he had been resisting arrest. Father heard that Halil had been gunned down in cold blood. That was the trouble in Kosovo – the truth was as remote as peace.

Mother's anxious voice cut across my thoughts. "Drita, dear, your father thinks it's not safe for you to go to school anymore. All that way on the bus alone . . . and you only fifteen."

It took a while for her words to sink in. All *what* way? Pec was only a few miles away. The trip took no longer than twenty minutes. "I could go with Father when he goes to work," I offered.

Father looked up sharply. "No, Drita! I never know where I'm going to be. The bus is the only way and it's no longer safe."

I felt a lump rising in my throat. "But I've bought all those books! And I've only just started my courses. At least let me finish this year. *Please!*"

Father was not moved. "There will be a time for school, Drita. But now there are more important things." He stood up and put a heavy arm around my shoulders. "Come on! Safe is better than sorry. Anyway, I've spoken to Dr. Gashi and he's going to give you private lessons. I told him you'd go there this evening to arrange things, and then . . ."

I stopped listening. Dr. Gashi, the retired teacher, lived on the other side of the crossroad. To get there I'd have to pass Zoran's house.

Perhaps studying with Dr. Gashi wouldn't be so bad after all.

Two

Zoran

Although Zoran Sakic and I had lived in the same village all our lives, until last summer the only thing we had in common was our age. We went to different schools and our families never met. The only time I remember them speaking was when Mr. Sakic asked Father to help him start his tractor. Father did so and was surprised when his bill was paid on time.

Last June I learned I had a place at a secondary school in Pec. No girl from our family had ever been to secondary school before. I was determined to do well, and most afternoons I went to a thicket in the fields behind our house to read. It was there, one day in early July, that my friendship with Zoran began.

I was sitting cross-legged on the grass, lost in my book, when a quiet voice interrupted me. "Interesting?" it asked.

Looking up, I saw a boy standing beside a tree watching me. I hadn't seen Zoran for some time and it took a few seconds before I recognized him. Dressed in jeans and a red checked shirt, he was more handsome than I remembered. I blushed and put down my book.

"Interesting?" he repeated.

"Yes," I replied defensively, "if you like that sort of thing."

"What is it?"

I showed him the cover. "History. The history of Yugoslavia."

He laughed. "History, Drita? You don't want to bother with that. It means nothing but trouble."

I glanced at him cautiously. "What do you mean?"

"You know what I mean. Serbs and Albanians – Kosovo – all the stupid fighting and killing – history's to blame, isn't it?"

I looked him in the eye. Yes, he meant it. Quite by chance, I seemed to have found someone who thought like me. And not just anyone, either. Zoran Sakic was a Serb.

I had never had a serious conversation with a Serb before. At first we talked cautiously about our families, then about Kosovo in general. Zoran agreed that Albanians and Serbs should be treated equally. "But," he frowned, "it doesn't help when you take up terrorism."

"Not *me!*" I replied sharply. "Anyway, the Kosovo

Liberation Army are freedom fighters, not terrorists." I had heard Muhamet use the same phrase a thousand times, although I had never used it myself before.

Zoran's dark eyes narrowed. "*Freedom fighters?*" he scoffed. "Killing makes someone free, does it?"

I was not used to being contradicted and started to get angry. "Listen, Zoran. I didn't say killing was right. It's just that the KLA use force to stop all of you from stealing our country."

"*Your country?* The Serbs came to Kosovo long before the Albanians."

"*Rubbish!* Everyone knows the Albanians go back to Roman times—"

"Listen, know-it-all," interrupted Zoran, now bright red, "I haven't come here for a history lesson."

Suddenly, I was struck by how ridiculous we sounded. "Sssh!" I hissed, holding up my hand as if I'd heard someone coming.

The color fled from Zoran's face. "What is it?" he whispered, obviously frightened by what would happen to him if he were found talking to an Albanian.

"Only us, Zoran," I grinned, "carrying on like a couple of boring politicians." I stepped forward and held out my hand. "No more stupid squabbles, OK?"

He grasped my hand firmly. "Sorry, Drita. Yes, friendship first. Above all."

"Above all," I nodded. I didn't mind when our handshake lasted a little longer than was necessary.

I saw Zoran six or seven more times that summer. We always met in the thicket, which we nicknamed our "parliament." When fall came and I started my new school, things got more difficult. We couldn't use the phone in case our families overheard. Instead, we kept in touch by leaving letters in a rusty milk can near the bridge at the bottom of the village.

I checked our secret mailbox every day on my way back from school. Someone might have seen me, but it was worth the risk. As Zoran said in one of his letters, "*We are the future, Drita. You and me, Albanian and Serb, good friends. It's the way it must be in Kosovo.*"

When I think now how innocent we were, it makes me cry.

Three

Dr. Gashi

As it was not yet dark, I was allowed to walk to Dr. Gashi's by myself. I promised to call when I had finished so Father or Muhamet could come and get me.

Zoran's house stood in a large compound near the crossroad. It was surrounded by a high brick wall topped with jagged pieces of broken glass. Across the entrance stood a pair of rusty iron gates secured with a large padlock. A mangy German Shepherd Dog glared at me suspiciously through the bars. There was no sign of Zoran or anyone else. Setting aside my disappointment, I walked quickly by and was soon knocking at Dr. Gashi's door.

Dr. Gashi had lost his job as a teacher several years earlier, when the Serb authorities had closed most Albanian schools. He now lived alone, surviving on his savings and what money he could get by giving private lessons.

His greeting was so old-fashioned it was almost funny. "Ah, Miss Binaku!" he exclaimed with a slight bow. "Good evening! You are well, I trust?"

"Very well, thanks, Dr. Gashi," I replied, stepping in out of the cold. "And you?"

"Who can honestly say they are well in these troubled times, Miss Binaku?" he sighed. "But it is God's will." When I did not reply, he nodded and looked over my shoulder. "I did not hear a car, Miss Binaku. Surely you did not walk through the mud?"

"I did, Dr. Gashi. It's not dark yet and I wanted some fresh air."

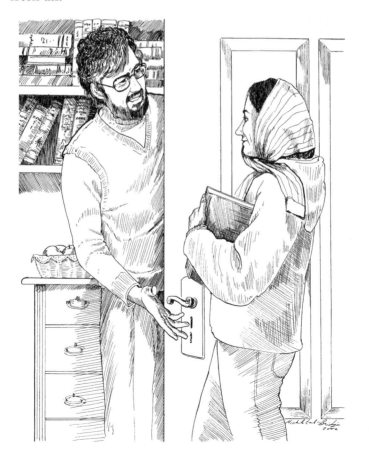

"Of course, Miss Binaku. A short walk down the lane for . . . *fresh air*. What a good idea!" His eyes twinkled with the hint of a smile.

Dr. Gashi agreed to help me with languages, literature, history, and geography. He apologized that he could not offer math and science. "Unfortunately, Miss Binaku," he explained, "I have always been more interested in people than things. I believe that if we learn about people, then things will look after themselves."

He rose and paced up and down the room trying to light his pipe. "I wish I were more practical. I can't even light my pipe!" He looked through the window into the gathering darkness. "As for my yard, it's a disgrace. Do you know of a young man who might like to earn a little money helping me? Perhaps your brother, or . . ." He left the sentence unfinished.

As he turned back into the room, I noticed that he had the same amused look on his face. I couldn't figure out Dr. Gashi at all.

Despite his odd ways, Dr. Gashi was a good teacher and I enjoyed my lessons with him. It was certainly better than being at home. The winter was cold and wet. With no school to go to, Rukie, Fatime, and Naser hung around the house getting in Mother's way. Usually they would have gone next door to spend time with Grandma, but she was unwell.

Every day on the BBC World Service we heard of fresh fighting between the Serbs and the KLA. My school in Pec, Father told me, had been burned down by a Serb gang calling itself the Thunder. Armed soldiers patrolled the streets day and night. Business was bad.

One evening, after Father had told us how a Serb officer had demanded that Father fix his exhaust for free, I finally asked the question that had been troubling me for ages. "If things are so bad, Father, how come we still have so much money?"

"It's nothing to do with you, Drita!" he snapped.

I was more surprised than upset. "That's not fair!" I cried. "I only asked. I'm not a little girl anymore, Father."

His face softened. "I'm sorry, Drita. I'm very on edge at the moment. We all are. If you really want to know, Uncle Ali helps us out. In return, I don't charge when I work on his cars."

Uncle Ali, Father's brother, owned a fleet of taxis. It made sense that Father should work for him. But what kind of work? A girl at school had once told me that passengers were not all that Uncle Ali's taxis carried. Good and bad, right and wrong – everything was confused. There was no black and white in Kosovo anymore, just a dirty gray fog of lies.

Four

Behind the Door

". . . and unless both sides attend these peace talks, NATO is prepared to use air strikes . . ."

Muhamet leaned over and switched off the radio. "Peace talks!" he said scornfully. "What's the use of talking to Serbs? They didn't keep their word in the past and they won't in the future. They're all liars." He threw himself into a chair and stared into the fire, still muttering fiercely.

I was sitting at the table, working at an English translation Dr. Gashi had given me. I glanced at Muhamet. He had been away from home for the past week, helping Uncle Ali. He looked tired and pale.

"Surely there's no harm in talking?" I suggested.

"Rubbish! What do you know about it, Drita? The Serbs understand only one thing – force! Kosovo must fight to be free."

"But Rugova says . . ."

"*Rugova!*" snarled Muhamet. "Pathetic! He's just an American puppet. The KLA haven't got any time for him at all."

This annoyed me. I quite liked gentle, intelligent Rugova, the Albanian leader who talked of peace, not war. "At least he doesn't support killing," I said.

Muhamet glared angrily at me. "Then he should! It's the only way."

"Would you kill someone, Muhamet?" I asked, realizing I knew the answer already.

"Of course!"

I returned to my translation. But I couldn't concentrate. What had Muhamet been doing while he was away? Could my own brother be in the KLA? If he was, then it was not only Muhamet, but the whole family, who would be in danger if the Serbs found out.

Two weeks later my fears were confirmed. I had gone to bed early to read. After about half an hour, needing to take notes, I came downstairs to get my pen and pad. As I approached the living room door, I paused and listened. Father, Muhamet, and Uncle Ali were deep in conversation.

". . . and I'll say I'm working for you as a driver, isn't that right, Uncle Ali?"

"Yes, Muhamet."

"But *is* it right, Muhamet?" asked Father. "You know what'll happen if you are caught. And it won't be just you that'll suffer."

"I won't get caught, Father. I'll pick up the stuff and be over the border in a couple of days. Then I'll hand over the cash to Uncle Ali and join up."

"Oh, God! Where's it all leading?" I heard Father sigh.

Then Uncle Ali spoke. "Listen, Sadik. If the Army needs money, then it's our job to get it. By any means we can. Your Muhamet's a good boy. If he wants to make the run, let him. There'll be something in it for you, too. You need the cash, don't you?"

"You know I do," Father replied.

"Good, it's decided then," said Uncle Ali. "Cheer up, Sadik! You'll be the father of a hero! Now, let's all have a cup of tea."

Hearing footsteps approaching the door, I turned and tiptoed back upstairs.

Safely back in bed, I lay there thinking over what I had heard. It sounded as if my whole family was mixed up in the "Army" – the KLA. Muhamet was going to join it. Uncle Ali was supporting it with money. And Father was also involved somehow, although less willingly. It almost seemed as if Uncle Ali was blackmailing him.

I went over the conversation again. There was one bit that still puzzled me. What was the "stuff" that Muhamet was going to pick up? And the cash? Would that come from selling the "stuff?" In the end I decided there could be only one answer: Uncle Ali was funding the KLA through smuggling and Muhamet and my father were helping him.

I was angry, upset, and confused. Everyone knew of the anti-Albanian racism of President Milosevic and his followers. But if Muhamet and Uncle Ali had their way, the Serbs would be driven out of Kosovo just as they wanted to drive us out. That wasn't right, either.

There must be a better way, I thought. If Zoran and I could talk, why couldn't others? I lay awake for ages, thinking through what I had heard and what it all meant. Finally, just before I dropped off to sleep, I made up my mind. Whatever the risk, I had to see Zoran again.

Five

Dr. Gashi's Surprise

The next morning I scribbled a quick note to Zoran asking to see him as soon as possible. I then told Mother I'd take the children for a walk. Naser was watching the video of *Titanic* that Uncle Ali had left and didn't want to come with us. I wanted to watch the video, too, but reckoned my own secret relationship was more important than the one in the film.

I bundled Fatime and Rukie into their outdoor clothes and, with my letter safe in the pocket of my ski jacket (another present from Uncle Ali), we went out into the muddy lane. On the right of the Zahac road, just before the bridge, stood a deserted Christian church. It had been built for Serb settlers who came to Toskik after World War I. They had not stayed long and their place of worship had soon fallen into disrepair. Birds and mice were the only congregation that gathered there now.

17

Our "mailbox" was hidden in brambles along the lower wall of the churchyard. To get Fatime and Rukie out of the way, I arranged a game of hide-and-seek. I closed my eyes and counted to fifty. Then, pretending to be looking for them, I went over to the milk can. I was surprised to find a letter already there. I fished it out and put mine in its place.

As soon as we got home, I went straight to the bathroom, locked the door, and took out the letter. Zoran normally wrote pages and pages. This time he had managed only a few lines.

"*Dear Drita,*" I read. "*Good news! The scholar and the laborer have the same master. See you there! Love, Zoran.*"

Wondering what he meant, I stuffed the note into my pocket and went to help Mother prepare lunch.

My next lesson with Dr. Gashi was on Thursday afternoon. That morning I heard that Serb and Albanian leaders had agreed to meet for peace talks in Rambouillet, France. I was therefore looking more cheerful than usual when Dr. Gashi opened his door.

"Good afternoon, Miss Binaku," he smiled. "You do look happy. Is it your birthday?"

"No, Dr. Gashi," I replied, hanging my jacket on a hook by the door. "I heard on the radio that peace talks are starting. It's good news, isn't it?"

"Maybe," he answered, feeling in his pocket for his pipe. "But don't expect too much, Miss Binaku. Talks usually work only when there has first been a change in people's hearts." He began stuffing tobacco into the bowl of his pipe. "But you never know. This time it may be different."

We began going through an essay I had written about the outbreak of World War I. After about a quarter of an hour, we were interrupted by a knock at the backdoor. Dr. Gashi excused himself and went to see who it was. I heard the door open and someone entering. Seconds later, Zoran walked into the room.

For once in my life I was lost for words. I looked first at Zoran, who was grinning from ear to ear, then at Dr. Gashi.

The teacher spoke first. "Miss Binaku, may I introduce Mr. Zoran Sakic? He has kindly agreed to come and help clean up my yard for me. I don't think his father approves, so, if you don't mind, I think this had better be a little secret between us."

"Of course," I stammered. "But how did you know . . . ?"

"So many questions, Miss Binaku!" said Dr. Gashi, his eyes gleaming with amusement. "You know I'm interested in wildlife? Well, last summer, while looking for butterflies, I saw this young man talking with a friend. They were in a thicket not far from your house. You probably know the place, Miss Binaku? It would be an ideal spot for a quiet read.

"Now, when I was wondering who might do odd jobs for me, I remembered Mr. Sakic. I bumped into him in the road the other day, and here he is. Please sit down. You look as if you could do with a cup of tea. I'll go and make one before we get on with our work."

With that, he walked out of the room, leaving Zoran and me staring at each other in confused delight.

Six

One of Us

If we had been in a movie, Zoran and I would have rushed into each other's arms the moment Dr. Gashi left the room. Instead, we were too embarrassed to do anything except laugh nervously.

"Why has he done this?" Zoran whispered.

I shrugged. "I've no idea, except that I think he's one of us."

"Meaning?"

"Before you came in, he said he thought there would be peace only when people's hearts had changed. Peace has to start with friendship between individuals, like us." I looked into Zoran's dark eyes and smiled. "Lucky us, eh?"

"Very lucky, yes!"

Dr. Gashi took a long time making tea. Before he returned, I explained to Zoran what I had learned about my family. A deep frown spread across his face. He was not surprised, he told me. His own father had been talking about what was going on. Zoran's Uncle Vidomir, a policeman in Pec, had warned them about Uncle Ali. He was being watched, which meant Muhamet probably was, too. If the peace talks failed, our families were going to be in the thick of it.

"And us?" I asked. "What can we do, Zoran?"

We were facing each other in the middle of the room. He took both my hands in his and said quietly, "All we can do, Drita, is what we believe is right and remain true to each other."

"Friendship first," I suggested, recalling his words at our first meeting, "even before family?"

"Above all."

That evening, when I thought how confident he had sounded, I felt a tiny pang of anxiety. I hoped he would never have to prove his words with deeds.

Although Zoran and I met several times at Dr. Gashi's house, he never once spoke openly about our friendship. The nearest he came was at the end of February, after we had heard that the peace talks had failed.

"What do you think will happen now, Dr. Gashi?" I asked.

"Things will take their course, Miss Binaku," he replied slowly, "and I fear more bloodshed. Much more. But you and your friendship must survive. It is the only way." After a short pause, he pointed with his pen at the map of France I had drawn for my geography homework. "Really, Miss Binaku, you must be more careful. Paris is not on the Loire River!"

Seven

Muhamet

By early March the BBC World Service was carrying daily reports of Serb soldiers and bandits driving Albanians from their homes. It was called "ethnic cleansing." The government television programs told a different story. They showed grizzly films of Serbs murdered by the KLA and said the army was winning its war against the terrorists.

One evening Mother and I watched a special report on the KLA. It concluded that the organization was funded by drug smugglers. I looked across at Mother when it finished. She was dabbing her eyes with a handkerchief.

We saw almost nothing of Muhamet now. When he did show up, he was like a different person. He was rude and aggressive, even to Mother and Father. I tried to stay out of his way, but it was not always possible.

Coming down to breakfast one morning, I found him sitting at the table working through a huge plate of eggs

Mother had cooked for him. His hands and unshaven face were filthy and he was eating as if he hadn't tasted food for a week.

"Morning, Muhamet," I said as cheerfully as I could. "Are you all right?"

He stopped eating and stared at me. There were huge dark rings under his eyes. "What do you mean?" he asked menacingly.

"I just asked if you were OK, that's all."

"Why shouldn't I be? What do you know, little Miss Serb lover?"

I felt my heart quicken. To hide my fear, I replied scornfully, "Serb lover? Come off it, Muhamet! I don't like Milosevic any more than you do."

"Rubbish! Everyone knows you're a Rugova supporter. All lovey-dovey while the Serbs carry on killing behind your back."

A wave of relief swept over me. For one dreadful moment I thought he had found out about Zoran. I put my hand on his shoulder. "Please don't let's argue, Muhamet. Please."

"OK," he shrugged and attacked his breakfast again. "But remember, Drita; all Serbs are scum. Especially the ones in this village. If you knew what I do about that Sakic lot, you'd soon change your tune." He ate in silence for a moment, then added, "But they won't get away with it much longer. We'll get them, Drita. You can be sure of that!"

Eight

Alone

M uhamet's boast that he'd "get" the Sakics put me in a panic. I couldn't think about anything else. Helping Fatime get dressed, I absentmindedly tried to shove her head through the sleeve of her pullover. Her squeals of laughter brought me back to reality, but only for a little while.

Should I take Muhamet's threat seriously? I remembered the wild look in his eyes and decided that I should. What then? If I told Zoran, his family might leave and I'd never see him again. I could be suspected of passing on the warning, too. But if I did nothing and the Sakics were attacked, even killed, then I would have Zoran's blood on my conscience for the rest of my life.

Mother didn't say much, but I knew she thought a lot about what was going on. While we were sorting through the laundry after breakfast, she suddenly said, "I know I shouldn't say this to you, Drita, but I'm frightened. I'm sure the Serbs will come to Toskik sooner or later. They do such terrible things, some of them. I can't bear the thought of anyone being hurt."

"We'll be OK if we stick together," I said, letting go of my end of the sheet we were folding and kissing her.

She looked at me with such sad eyes. "Do you think so, Drita? Maybe you and the other children should go away now, before anything happens. I'd rather be separated from you than see you come to any harm."

Mother's remark made up my mind for me. When we had finished putting away the laundry, I scribbled a quick note to Zoran and took my younger brother and sisters out for a walk. As I dropped the envelope into the milk can, I felt as if I were leaving my heart there, too.

Three days later, on my way to Dr. Gashi's, I noticed a large blue truck parked in the Sakics' compound. Men were loading it with furniture. As I watched, Zoran and another man came out of the house carrying a sofa. I stopped for a few seconds, hoping he would look up and see me. But he was too wrapped up in what he was doing to notice me.

Later, Dr. Gashi said his "handyman" was leaving the village and wouldn't be coming around anymore. "I'll miss him," he said kindly, "and I guess you will, too." My teacher was big on understatement.

Spring used to be my favorite season. I loved to feel the warm wind blowing from the south. I loved the rushing of the river swollen with melted snow. I loved the fresh green of the fields, the buds, and the sound of birdsong. But this year it was different. The natural world seemed to mock us. "Look at me," it laughed. "I am fruitful and full of hope. While I burst with new life, you shrivel with new death!"

As the weather became drier, the Serbs stepped up their ethnic cleansing. In the north and east, we heard, whole villages were being cleared of their Albanian inhabitants. The houses were burned and the people herded like cattle toward the borders with Macedonia or Albania.

There were reports of killings, too. It was usually men suspected of supporting the KLA who suffered. But sometimes whole families were slaughtered. Or so we were told. One of the worst things was not knowing what was really happening.

To my relief, no one had paid much attention when the Sakics left. It was more or less expected. Mother said it was a good thing because it meant less chance of trouble. Some Albanian families moved out, too, leaving parts of the village as lifeless as an old movie set. Meanwhile, our life went on. I still had my lessons with Dr. Gashi, Father still went to work in Pec, and Mother continued with her endless cooking, washing, and cleaning.

On March 15, a new round of peace talks began in France. We kept the radio on all day, and for a time the news was good. The only impasse was whether foreign peacekeepers should be allowed to enter Kosovo. The Albanians were prepared to accept them; the Serbs were not. Kosovo was part of their country, they said, and no foreigners had a right to interfere there.

I didn't care whose country it was, as long as there was peace. Then Zoran would be able to come home.

Nine

The Road

The peace talks broke down on March 19. Five days later, NATO began its air attacks on Serbia. I remember the date – Wednesday, March 24 – because it was two days before Rukie's eleventh birthday. On Thursday I was supposed to be going into Pec with Father and Mother to buy her a present but the trip was canceled because of the war.

Instead, in the morning Father went into town alone to buy food and see what was happening. He promised to get a present for Rukie if he could. By lunchtime he had not returned and we started to get worried. When he was still not back by mid-afternoon, Naser and I decided to walk down to the main road to wait for him there.

Coming over the hill above the bridge, we stood and stared in amazement. There was always some traffic on the road, but today it was jammed solid. Cars, trucks, tractors, and every other type of vehicle stretched as far as the eye could see. They were all moving away from Pec. Most were piled high with belongings – suitcases, bundles, bedding, even chairs and tables.

Naser and I sat down on the grass beside the lane and watched the dismal procession in silence for a few minutes. Then he asked, "What's going on, Drita? Where are they all going?"

"I don't know," I replied. "But I can guess. They're getting out of Pec and going somewhere safer."

"Why?"

"The Serbs have probably driven them out. You know, it's what they call 'ethnic cleansing' – getting rid of the Albanians."

For a while Naser sat fiddling with the laces of his

sneakers, thinking. "Does that mean we'll have to leave, too?" he asked eventually.

"Maybe. But I hope not."

"So do I," said Naser. "I hate long trips. They make me carsick."

Father arrived home just before dark. He had been stuck in the traffic for hours and looked tired and depressed. "And the shopping?" Mother asked. "Did you manage to get Rukie's present?"

Father shook his head. "Sorry, Zarife. No shopping and no presents. And there won't be any, either."

He explained how the police had stopped him before he got into the town and told him to go home. Wanting to see what was happening, he had left his car farther up the road and sneaked past the police on foot. The town was in chaos. The streets were crawling with Serb soldiers and thugs were going from house to house, ordering all Albanians to leave before nightfall. Some Albanian shops had been looted. Serb thugs shot one man in cold blood when he refused to let them into his bar.

Before he left, Father went to see if Uncle Ali was OK. He couldn't get near the house. The front door had been smashed in and there was an armed guard outside. When he asked a neighbor what had happened, the man just shrugged. He knew nothing, he said. It was better that way.

*   *   *

31

The next three weeks were unreal. Occasionally we saw aircraft high overhead and once we heard the distant rumble of heavy artillery. But apart from not being able to leave the village, the war passed us by. In the quiet of the early morning it was difficult to believe it was actually happening.

Of course, we had only to switch on the TV or radio to know that this was not true. According to the government, NATO bombs and missiles were killing innocent citizens every night. But the Serb army, its commander declared proudly, was almost untouched. Foreign broadcasters told a different story. They said Serb factories had suffered massive damage and many tanks and guns had been put out of action. I read somewhere that this muddle of truth and untruth is called the "fog of war." It struck me as a good image.

The "fog" lifted from Toskik on April 17. We were just clearing away the lunch things when we heard the rapid rat-atat of machine-gun fire. Shortly afterward we saw smoke billowing up from the direction of the bridge. After dark one of our neighbors, Mr. Halili, called. Members of the Thunder gang had paid Toskik a visit that afternoon, he said. They had driven the Zeme family from their compound at the edge of the village and set fire to their homes.

Our nightmare had begun.

Ten

The Last Post

After the Thunder's attack we spent most of the time indoors. When we did go out, we never went far and peered suspiciously at every car that entered the village. Father cancelled my lessons with Dr. Gashi. By day we were nervous and irritable. At night we slept uneasily, awakened by the slightest sound.

It was during this period that Muhamet called for the last time. He appeared like a ghost, stayed a few hours, then glided away into the darkness. There was no need to ask him what he had been doing: a gleaming Kalashnikov leaning against the wall by the fire told us clearly enough. He was just as dirty and gaunt as on his last visit, but he had lost his aggressiveness. Seeing him sprawled out in a chair, utterly exhausted, I felt sorry for him. He was like a child who had been playing all day and was too tired to go upstairs to bed.

Father and he discussed what we should do. We could abandon our house and flee, as several neighbors had already done, or we could stay and risk another visit from the Thunder. Muhamet said a gang did not often come to the same village twice, so we were probably all right where we were. Father trusted Muhamet's judgment and decided we were staying put.

The first sign that Father's decision was wrong came on the morning of April 19. I was outside, watching the children playing, when Naser suddenly pointed to the sky. "Hey, Drita!" he cried. "Look – a fire!"

I followed the direction of his hand. A column of gray smoke was rising into the sky away to the north.

Alerted by the noise, Father came outside to join us. "That's across the valley," he said, staring at the sinister cloud, "somewhere near the village of Pavlan. I hope those

poor souls aren't getting a visit. If they are, then the Thunder is still around." He shook his head and went back into the house.

I sat watching the smoke for a long time. The mention of Pavlan had brought on a fresh wave of sadness. It was where Zoran's cousins, the Popovics, lived. I wondered where Zoran was now and what he was doing. I missed his voice, his smile, his letters so much.

Then a thought struck me. What if the Sakics had gone only as far as the Popovics' house at Pavlan? If they had, then Zoran might have managed to get a letter to our mailbox. The more I thought about it, the more obsessed I became with the idea. Somehow I had to check the milk can.

None of us were allowed to go as far as the church now. I couldn't sneak out without being noticed, either. My only hope was to find someone to look in the can for me. But who?

"I've got some books to return to Dr. Gashi," I told Father. "Would it be OK for me to walk there with the children?"

Father agreed but only if he came, too. When we arrived, he said Dr. Gashi wouldn't appreciate an invasion of dirty feet. While he stayed outside with the children, I went into the house alone.

I didn't mention to Dr. Gashi why I wanted him to look in the can for me. He didn't exactly agree to do so, either. But we both understood each other. As Zoran and I had discovered, Dr. Gashi was one of us.

The next morning I found a large brown envelope that had been pushed under the door during the night. It was addressed to Miss Drita Binaku. Underneath was written, *"Some notes I meant to give you on peacemaking. I hope they will be useful. H. Gashi."*

After breakfast I took the envelope up to my room and opened it. Inside were handwritten notes on the Treaty of Versailles, 1918. Nothing else. In my disappointment, I tried to force open the envelope. It was stiffer than I expected. Examining it carefully, I found a sheet of brown paper pasted along the inside to make a hidden pocket. In the pocket was a second, smaller envelope.

"Is everything OK, Drita?" called Mother from the kitchen when she heard my whoop of joy.

"Fine, thanks!" I called back, shoving Zoran's letter inside my sweater. "It's just something Dr. Gashi sent me. I've been waiting for it for ages!"

Eleven

The Thunder

*D*earest Drita, I read. *You're amazing, beautiful, brave, clever – AND you saved my life! AND my father's and brothers'! You are a LEGEND!!!*

I didn't know what to do when I got your note about what your brother said. Luckily, my brother Sherif said he heard the KLA were in the area and we'd probably be a target. Then, by chance, our cousins in Pavlan – the Popovics – called and asked us to go over there. Strength in numbers, they said. So I made up a story about seeing suspicious-looking men in the woods above the farm – and that decided it. We packed up right away and moved to Pavlan.

How are you? I think about you every minute of every day and pray you're OK. I hate it here. I have to share a room with my awful cousins, Zvonmir and Sreko. All they do is go on about how useless NATO is, how the Serbs are the best fighters in the world, and how they can't wait for the next ethnic cleansing. (They're both in some anti-Albanian gang.) It makes me sick. But all I can do is grin like an idiot and pretend I agree. If I told them how I really feel, they'd beat me up or hand me over to the police as a traitor. Actually, I sometimes think that would be best. At least it would be honest. But it would give the idea that we – that's us! – support NATO or the KLA, which we don't. Oh, Drita! Isn't it hard trying to change the world with handshakes and kisses?! I wish I could do something useful.

I'm going to try to get this letter to our mailbox tomorrow. I'm borrowing Sreko's motorbike and – if I don't fall off – I'll get down to the Toskik bridge. It'll be really tempting to continue up to the village. I'll zoom up to your house – skid to a halt – you'll run out – jump on the back of the bike – and we'll roar off to . . .

Dream on, sweet Zoran! I thought. Dream on!

There were two more pages, saying again how much he missed me, and hoping I'd be able to reply. But I mustn't take risks, he insisted: *It would be the worst thing in the world if we were found out, dearest Drita. Our secret must survive. It's the seed for the New Kosovo after the war . . .*

"After the war" – how easily he wrote it! Had he really thought about what might have happened by then? The war wasn't just about moving house or TV news or NATO planes overhead. It was Zoran's family wanting to drive out mine, and Muhamet, twisted with hatred and anger, wanting to kill the Sakics. It was living in terror, praying to be left alone. It was a dark blanket beneath which there was no tomorrow.

The thugs paid us a second visit on April 21, the day after I got Zoran's letter.

They came suddenly, roaring around the village in four-wheel-drive trucks, horns blaring, shooting pointlessly into the morning sky. As soon as we heard the noise, we ran inside, closed the shutters, and locked the doors. Mother and I hid in the cupboard under the stairs with my little brother and sisters. Father waited in the living room, alone.

It was so dark in the cupboard we couldn't even see each other's faces. We sat on the floor, holding the children's hands and telling them there was nothing to worry about because no one could find us in such a secret place. They were not deceived. I had often read of the smell of fear, but never knew what it was till then. It rose from our bodies and spread through the dusty darkness until it filled the whole cupboard. My mouth went dry. Rukie and Fatime whimpered like puppies.

We heard a crash as the front door was kicked in. There was shouting and suddenly the cupboard door was flung open. The blunt nose of a rifle was pushed toward us. Behind it appeared a man whose demon eyes shone out of a face disguised with blacking, like a coal miner's.

"Get out!" he ordered. "Unless you want to be burned alive!"

Twelve

Face to Face

Still holding each other tight by the hand, we stumbled
out of the cupboard, past the broken front door and
onto the grass beside the road. Father was lying on the
ground with a group of men standing over him. One of
them was jangling a bunch of keys in his hand and
laughing.

For a second I thought Father was dead. But as I
watched, he got slowly to his feet and came over to join
us. His face was as pale as milk and he was breathing
heavily. "Don't be frightened," he whispered, "they're
only thieves. Just give them what they want. Whatever you
do – don't argue."

Two open trucks were parked in the middle of the road
in front of our house. In the back sat armed men in
combat uniforms hiding behind blackened faces. Their
gleaming eyes and pink mouths reminded me of the devil's
servants in medieval pictures of hell, grinning as they led

their victims to everlasting fire. I couldn't believe such fiends were just simple thieves.

The man with the keys took a few steps toward us. It was clear by his walk and voice that he was not much older than twenty. "Time you all contributed to the war, right? The old man's given us his car," he jangled the keys and I recognized the familiar Mercedes sign on the chain, "and now it's your turn. What've you got? Jewelry? Watches? Just hand it over and there won't be any trouble, OK?"

Without a word, Mother took off her watch and the heavy gold chain from around her neck. The man grabbed them and pointed to her hands. "Come on, what about them rings?"

"I'm afraid they won't come off. My fingers have swollen—"

"You mean I've got to cut 'em off?" He reached for the knife that hung at his side.

"None of that, Sreko!" ordered an older man sitting behind the wheel of the first truck. "You've got enough. Hurry up."

"Sure thing, Dad – I mean Captain Popo," mocked the younger man. His name sounded vaguely familiar. I looked at him closely, trying to figure out the features behind the blacking.

He noticed my look and snarled, "What are you staring at, girl?"

I know I should have kept quiet, but something inside me refused. "Nothing," I replied, "except your face."

"Drita!" snapped Mother. "Be quiet!"

The man's eyes narrowed. "Oh? Drita is it?" he sneered, looking me up and down. I was glad I was wearing only my jeans and a plain sweatshirt. "So what are you going to give me then, Drita?"

How I hated him! He stood for everything I detested: vulgarity, thuggery, cruelty. Without thinking, I replied sarcastically, "I've got lots of things you'd like, Sreko." His eyes widened. "Paper, pens, books—"

He lunged forward and grabbed the front of my sweatshirt, almost lifting me off the ground. "Don't mess with me, girl!"

"Leave her alone, Sreko, for God's sake!" called the captain. "What's the problem?"

Sreko slowly let go of me and turned toward the truck. "She says she's going to give us her books!"

The gang roared with laughter. One of them cried out, "Better take them then, Sreko. We'll give them to Zoran – he's always got his nose stuck in some book!"

The mention of Zoran struck me like an electric shock. My mind went blank. Without a word, I handed over my watch and the gold and silver bracelet my parents had given me for my twelfth birthday.

42

As the thief took them, he leaned forward and muttered, "Stupid cow! You won't be so lucky next time."

Watching them drive off up the road, taking Father's car with them, I tried to make sense of what had happened. It was almost unbelievable. Sreko must have been Zoran's eldest cousin and the truck driver Zoran's uncle. Now that they had finished with us, they would go home and show off their loot. Zoran would recognize my watch and bracelet at once. Sreko would probably make fun of what had happened, too.

For a few moments I was too upset to move. Then, as I turned to follow the others back into the house, I noticed Mother looking at me strangely. Our eyes met.

"Be careful, Drita, darling," she said quietly. "Please be careful!"

Thirteen

The Bracelet

Danger had swept upon us like a tide. First it had washed against distant settlements, then risen to the outskirts of our own village. Now it had reached our house, threatening our family and possessions. Its arrival had brought us face to face with our enemy for the first time. We had felt their hatred and seen their anger. Both were merciless.

The gang blew up the substation as they left the village, leaving us without running water or electricity. We were forced to live like peasants, drawing water from wells by hand, cooking on wood fires, and lighting the house with oil lamps or candles. Fortunately, Mother had built up supplies for such an emergency.

Other villagers were less fortunate and a committee was set up to share food and other essentials. The committee also organized a twenty-four-hour watch on the track from the main road. The lookouts, based in the tower of the ruined church, were to ring its rusty bell if anyone suspicious approached. On hearing the signal, we would flee to the woods above the village.

Fear changed our attitude toward NATO. Now that we had no car, its distant aircraft became messengers of hope. Apart from trying to reach Macedonia or Albania on foot, our main hope was that NATO land forces would attack before the Thunder returned.

Our only link with the outside world was the radio. When the batteries on my radio ran out, we relied on Mr. Halili's car radio. Each evening Father and I went over to his house to catch the foreign news. We sat in the back seat and Mr. and Mrs. Halili sat in the front, as if we were going for an evening drive, and listened eagerly to reports of bombings and the buildup of NATO forces in Albania. But there was no news of the expected invasion. The commanders were waiting until they were sure of victory, said one correspondent. I wondered whether he realized what the delay meant for families like ours, waiting, terrified that the enemy might return.

The ringing of the church bell announced the Thunder's third visit. But before we had time to gather our belongings and get out, the trucks had entered the village and parked in the middle of the road about a hundred feet below our house.

"Don't worry," blared a voice through a loudspeaker, "just a routine visit."

I was reminded of the Nazi guards who had reassured Jews going to the gas chambers, telling them they had nothing to fear.

The voice demanded five hundred American dollars as a "war tax" from the head of every household. Watching from an upstairs window, I saw dejected figures leave their houses, walk slowly over to the trucks, and hand over their life's savings. Father paid twice, once for himself and once for his parents. For some reason this annoyed the commander, the same "Captain Popo" who had led their last visit. He drove up to my grandparents' house, ordered them out, and threw a grenade through the window. Half an hour later the home they had shared together for forty-five years was just a smoldering ruin. They were given my room and I moved in with Rukie and Fatime.

At about four o'clock the following morning I was awakened by a single gunshot. My sisters stirred but did not wake up. Going into my parents' room, I found Father standing at the open window with his shotgun in his hand.

"Thought I heard someone prowling around outside," he growled, "but it was probably only a goat. Whatever it was, it's gone now. Forget it, Drita, and go back to sleep."

I lay in bed listening to the sound of the children's

breathing and wondering what Father had heard. Could it have been Muhamet on one of his secret visits? I was so worried that Father might have shot his own son that at first light I dressed, sneaked downstairs, and went out through the back door.

I soon found the patch of torn grass not far from the house where the shot had landed. To my relief, there was no blood or other evidence that someone or something had been hit. But as I turned to go back indoors, my eye was caught by something shiny pinned to the washline.

It was the bracelet I had handed over to the Thunder eight days earlier.

Fourteen

Mrs. Zarife Binaku

When I got back to the house, I was startled to find Mother already in the kitchen. "Oh!" I exclaimed, trying hard to hide my confusion. "I didn't expect you to be up so early."

She looked at me warily. "I might say the same of you, Drita," she replied. "What have you been up to at this hour of the morning?"

"I went to see if Father hit anything when he fired out of the window last night. I was worried it might have been Muhamet."

Mother's broad face crumpled into a frown. "I was thinking the same, Drita. But it wasn't Muhamet, was it?"

"No. Well, I don't know. But how do you know it wasn't?"

She gave a half-smile and leaned back heavily against the sink with her hands resting on the rim of the draining board. "Well, he didn't call out, which he would have if

Father had shot at him and missed. And he's not lying out there dead or wounded, either." She turned her head toward the window. For the first time I noticed that the shutters were open, giving a clear view of the land at the back of the house.

I felt my heartbeat quicken. "Then you saw—"

"I don't know what I saw, Drita, darling. And I don't want to know, either." She held out her hands toward me. "Come over here, please."

I did as she asked.

"Listen, Drita," she began, closing her thick arms around me so that I felt like a little child again, "I didn't go to school and I don't understand politics. I was brought up to be loyal to my husband and my family and to look after them. That's all. I cannot have secrets from your father, so I don't want to know any." She started gently stroking the back of my head. "But I have noticed things, of course. All mothers do. And I tried to warn you after the argument with that thug who took your bracelet."

I tried to lift my head but she eased it back against the soft pillow of her shoulder.

"No, don't say anything, Drita. I'm sure you're not disloyal. But I also know you're a headstrong girl. You always knew best, even when you were little. So take care. Please, Drita."

Even now I can feel the warmth of my mother's body and hear the earnestness in her voice. It was one of the turning points of my life. For the first time I saw her not as my mother but as Mrs. Zarife Binaku, wife of Sadik Binaku, mother of KLA soldier Muhamet Binaku. I knew there were some things I would never now be able to tell her because she would not understand.

"Thank you," I said quietly, kissing her on both cheeks. "I won't forget what you said, ever. And I promise I won't let you down." I took a deep breath. "Now, I might as well do something useful. What can I do to help?"

Mother eased herself off the rim of the sink. "Well, since there isn't any laundry to be brought in, you could light the fire. We could both do with a cup of coffee, couldn't we?"

The village was left in peace for two weeks. During that time I wondered endlessly about the mysterious reappearance of my bracelet. There seemed only two possibilities. One was that some member of the Thunder had returned it. But why? I couldn't think of a sensible reason. That meant Zoran had somehow gotten hold of the bracelet and brought it back himself. Perhaps it was a way of apologizing for the behavior of his cousin and letting me know he was still around. It was just the sort of crazy, romantic thing he would do.

The more I thought about it, the more I came to believe that was what had happened. It meant, of course, that my own father had tried to shoot my best friend! In case Zoran came again, I took to leaving the shutters of our room slightly open at night. I hoped I might hear him before Father did and warn him off. The plan worked, but not in the way I expected. It was not Zoran's life I saved, but Father's.

Fifteen

The Warning

The nightmare became reality on May 18. At about two o'clock in the morning, I was awakened by someone outside calling my name. The voice was familiar. When I realized what was happening, I was seized with panic. What on earth did the boy think he was doing? Was he trying to get shot? I climbed out of bed and looked out of the window.

A shadowy figure was standing under the window of my old room, now occupied by my grandparents. I remembered how, months ago, I had described our house to Zoran and told him where my room was. I glanced anxiously at the shutters of my old room and those of my parents. They were both still closed.

"Zoran?" I called quietly. The figure turned and started running toward me. Relief and happiness surged through me when I recognized the familiar features in the moonlight. "I've changed rooms, Zoran," I whispered. "What on earth—?"

"Drita, listen!" he interrupted hoarsely. "It's really important. I've got to speak you. And your family. You must let me in!"

"Let you in? My father would shoot you!"

"If he doesn't listen to me, it's he who'll be shot. You must believe me, Drita. Wake him up, please, then open the door!" Zoran's voice, normally so calm and cheerful, rasped with anxiety.

Telling Zoran to stay where he was, I threw a blanket around my shoulders and ran to my parents' room. At the door, I hesitated. Surely it couldn't be some sort of trap? Rejecting the idea, I went in and woke them up. I was unsure quite what to say and gabbled about someone outside with a very urgent message about Father being shot.

Father swore. "Rubbish, Drita!" he grunted, groping for his shotgun under the bed. "It's that prowler again. I'll get him this time!"

I didn't wait to argue. Rushing downstairs in my bare feet, I unbolted the back door and went outside. Zoran was still standing under my window. I called to him and, after a quick hug, led him back into the house. My parents had lit an oil lamp and come downstairs. Father was in the middle of the room, pushing a cartridge into the breech of his gun.

"What the devil do you think you're doing?" he growled when he saw who it was. "Out of the way, Drita!

Let me take a shot at him." He snapped his gun shut and raised the barrel.

Zoran let go of my hand and stepped forward. "Don't shoot, Mr. Binaku," he said calmly. "This is not a trick. I come in friendship – and with terrible news, I'm afraid."

As Father hesitated, Mother let out a cry of horror. "Oh, no! It's Muhamet, isn't it?" She covered her face with her hands. "Please say it isn't!" she begged.

"I'm afraid it is, Mrs. Binaku," said Zoran softly. Father lowered his gun, put an arm around Mother's shoulders, and led her to a chair. I remained standing, hardly able to believe what was happening.

"We have almost no time," Zoran went on. "Listen to me, please, then make up your own minds. It's the best I can do. Yesterday morning Muhamet was captured in the woods near Pavlan and handed over to the Thunder. He was taken to a barn on the Popovic's farm and tortured horribly . . ." Zoran did not know exactly what Muhamet had said before he died, but it was enough to condemn the whole Binaku family. In response, the Popovics and their Thunder assistants were going to carry out a revenge attack on Toskik at dawn.

When Zoran had finished, Father asked quietly, "But why, Zoran Sakic? Why do you want to help us?"

Zoran shrugged. "All my life I have dreamed of doing something noble, Mr. Binaku. This may be my only chance. I want to play my part in building a country that's fit for us to live in."

"Us?"

Zoran glanced across at me. A puzzled look crossed Father's face but he said nothing. Five minutes later, Zoran had disappeared into the night. Father turned to me and said, "I've learned a lot tonight, Drita. I think we'd better have a chat about it one day, don't you? When the war is over."

"Yes, Father," I replied, wiping away my tears, "when the war is over."

Sixteen

Only a Matter of Time

I had never before thought of my father as a frightened man. But as I watched him twisting his hands and staring anxiously into the darkness, I realized he was afraid. He was afraid for himself and for his family. He was also afraid of making a decision.

I suggested we should all go into hiding in the woods. This proved impossible because Mother, beside herself at the news of Muhamet's death, refused to leave the house. As my grandparents were not fit enough to live in the open, we finally decided Father should go alone.

"What about the neighbors?" I asked. "Surely we must warn them also."

"And if the Thunder turns up and finds the village deserted, won't they suspect something – someone?" replied Father.

By "someone," of course, he meant Zoran, although he couldn't bring himself to mention the name. I decided to leave it that way. "He will have thought of that," I suggested. "He must want to save as many people as possible."

"Even if those Thunder thugs find out he's betrayed them?"

"They won't find out. He's too clever." I hoped my pride in Zoran was not condemning him to horrible punishment.

Father agreed to warn as many families as he could when he left. Tragically, however, we had talked for too long. When he pushed open the patched-up front door, it was already beginning to get light. We watched from the doorway as he began crossing the road toward the Halilis' house.

He hadn't gone more than a couple of steps before he stopped and stood still, listening. From far down in the valley came the sound of vehicles approaching the village. Father turned to us, his face a mask of panic, then turned and ran around the house toward the fields and the woods beyond.

Unlike their previous visits, the Thunder seemed to have planned this one carefully. As six trucks swept up and down the lanes, summoning everyone to leave their houses and gather at the crossroad, thugs in two jeeps drove into the fields and farmyards, shooting every animal they saw.

Whatever else happened, the farmers of Toskik were ruined.

We walked down to the crossroad in two groups. Mother went ahead with Rukie and Fatime while Naser and I followed with our grandparents. Neither of them seemed to understand fully what was going on. Grandpa asked me several times why everyone was going for a walk before breakfast.

As two trucks patroled the village, shooting into the roofs of houses and herding the villagers toward the center, the other four had parked across the entrances to the crossroads. Everyone had to pass one of them to get to the assembly point. As they did so, the gangs collected

their identity papers and examined them.

"Hey, Captain Popo!" called the man who took Mother's papers. "It's the Binakus!"

The captain jumped down from the open back of the truck and grabbed Rukie firmly by the arm. "Where's your father, girl?" he demanded.

Rukie stared at him, too terrified to speak. The man shook her violently and yelled, "Are you deaf, child? I said where's your father?" Rukie burst into tears.

Struggling to control my anger, I went up to him and said as calmly as I could, "Excuse me, but Father went into Pec yesterday to see if he could buy fuel. He went on foot and hasn't come back yet."

The man's eyes glared at me out of his blackened face. "Oh, yes? Well he's the lucky one, isn't he?"

I can hardly bear to describe what happened next. When everyone had been gathered together, the captain explained that the whole village was being punished for sheltering "terrorist traitors" from the Binaku family. The crowd stirred uneasily. Captain Popovic then singled out twelve men and ordered them to be led away to the Gecis' compound, about two hundred feet beyond the crossroad. After a short silence, we heard several long bursts of gunfire.

Mr. Halili was among those who had been taken away. So was Grandpa.

At the sound of the shooting, Mother fell to her knees in the road and started weeping again. "God have mercy on us!" she sobbed. "The children will be next, I know! It's only a matter of time!"

Seventeen

The Traitor

I watched the execution squad amble slowly back to the crossroad. They were laughing and joking. Was this how all killers behaved, I wondered, hiding their guilt behind exaggerated jollity? One of them said something to the captain, who nodded and pointed to the back of one of the trucks. Three of the squad lifted out heavy, metal gas cans and carried them, two men to a can, back to the Gecis' compound. Shortly afterward, the scene of the crime was engulfed in flames and thick black smoke.

Those of us who were left huddled together in family groups, sitting or lying on the dusty road. Hardly anyone spoke. Mother rocked backward and forward, cradling the sleeping Fatime in her lap. Grandma, speaking very softly, told Rukie and Naser a story about a shepherd boy who, long ago, had fallen in love with a princess. Sitting slightly apart from the others, I scratched idle patterns in the dirt with my finger. My mind was a clouded screen on which images from my past flitted like clips from old movies.

At one point Mrs. Halili came over and squatted down beside me. "You mustn't blame yourselves, Drita," she said. "It wasn't your fault."

I glanced into her drawn, tear-stained face and nodded. "Thank you, Mrs. Halili. I'm very sorry. I really am. If only . . ." I couldn't finish the sentence. There were so many "if onlys," all of them pointless. As Mrs. Halili walked away, I started to cry. My tears dissolved like summer rain in the dust at my feet. The sun slid above the horizon and hung in the still sky, a huge, angry orange.

For about an hour the Thunder gang lounged around, smoking and chatting among themselves. The captain appeared increasingly anxious, as if unsure what to do next. From time to time he tried unsuccessfully to get through to someone on the radio. His obvious irritation pleased me.

Eventually, at about eight o'clock, we heard a motor-bike turn off the main road and begin the climb to the village. I was reminded of how Zoran had borrowed his cousin's motorbike to deliver his last letter to me. My stomach ached with the anguish of the memory.

The motorbike come to a halt near the truck that

blocked the road leading down to the church. The rider got off awkwardly and leaned his machine against a wall. His face was blacked over and he was wearing the same military-style combat clothes as the rest of the gang.

Wondering why he had come, I watched him talking to his colleagues. One of them pointed toward the captain and the messenger began walking around the edge of the villagers toward him.

My heart gave a sudden jump. The young man's build and walk were all too familiar. I stared in disbelief as he drew nearer. From time to time he turned his head and searched the crowd, as if looking for someone. When he was almost at Captain Popovic's truck, no more than ten feet away from me, he turned again. For an instant our eyes met.

It was Zoran. I looked away, sick with disappointment. He made no sign of having recognized me and was soon talking earnestly with his new commander.

Nothing mattered anymore. Now that Zoran had betrayed me, what price "friendship first?" I should have listened to my doubts after his confident promise at Dr. Gashi's. Obviously, he had felt guilty about warning us and joined up with his Serb family. But why such a swift change? Why had he sided with the murderers only hours after alerting us? In the end I decided such questions were useless. All I knew was that Zoran, my once dearest friend, was in league with killers. He was a traitor. I did not want to have anything to do with him ever again.

Although I refused to look at Zoran as he talked with his uncle, I couldn't help overhearing snatches of their conversation. They seemed to be arguing about what to do with us. Zoran had brought orders that the captain didn't like. Eventually, the older man exclaimed in a loud voice, obviously intended for everyone to hear, "OK, Zoran, I believe you. But I don't like it, I don't mind telling you. We'll do it. But you accept full responsibility."

Eighteen

Exodus

The captain summoned three of his men to him. After a brief chat, they walked off in the direction of the farm buildings beyond the burned-out mosque. Not long afterward, we heard the sound of engines and the men reappeared driving tractors. Each tractor was pulling a flat, four-wheeled hay wagon. The crowd moved uneasily aside as the vehicles drove around the trucks and halted in a line across the middle of the crossroad.

With much shouting and swearing, the thugs ordered all the women and children to climb onto the wagons. After I had helped the rest of the family aboard the leading one, I put my foot on the wheel to climb up myself. As I did so, someone behind me shouted, "Oi! Not that one! She's not going anywhere!"

I recognized the voice immediately. It was Zoran's cousin, Sreko, the man who had stolen my watch and bracelet. I took my foot off the wheel and turned around.

"My old pal Drita, isn't it?" he sneered. "The fresh one. I reckon it's time I taught you a lesson, darling." He raised a hand to hit me.

The events of the morning had drained my will to resist. I took a step back and lifted my hands to shield my face. As I did so, the sleeves of my sweater slipped up my arms. There, gleaming in the early morning light, was my bracelet.

Sreko stared in amazement. "What the—" he exclaimed, lowering his fist. "Where did you get that bracelet?"

I opened my mouth but no words came. I cowered back until my shoulders pressed against the side of the wagon.

Sreko followed, his face close to mine. "I said, where did you get that bracelet?"

"It's one of a pair we gave her for her twelfth birthday. If you remember, you took the other one." It was Mother, somehow roused from her despair by the threat to yet another member of her family. Through red, puffy eyes she glared down at Sreko, daring him to challenge her.

"Is that so?" he said slowly, trying to cover his confusion. "Then I'll have that one, too." Without a word, I took off the bracelet and handed it to him. "Right, as I was saying, it's time you learned some manners."

At that moment a whistle sounded and the wagon lurched forward. Without thinking, I turned and threw myself upward. Friendly hands lifted me to safety. Lying on the wagon floor, I saw Sreko running alongside us, yelling at the driver to stop. After a few strides, someone grabbed him and pulled him back. The two men struggled for a while before they were separated by their colleagues. As they stood back, I saw that the second man was Zoran.

We drove slowly past the reeking, smoking ruins of the Gecis' compound, over the bridge before turning left along the Pec road. We made a strange convoy. The jeeps, one at the front and one at the rear, acted as escorts. Each was fitted with a heavy machine gun, so there was no chance of escape by jumping from the wagons. Between the jeeps came the three ancient tractors, chugging along with their cargoes of wretched humanity.

It was a hot day. To keep off the sun, the women covered themselves and their children with their shawls. From a distance the wagons must have appeared loaded with bundles of billowing cloth. We were hungry, humiliated by the lack of a toilet, and desperately thirsty. Babies cried incessantly. Fatime, like many of the younger children, either slept or begged Mother for a drink. When not soothing their distressed children, most of the adults traveled in silence. I sat with my legs over the side of the wagon trying to come to terms with what had happened.

After about half an hour we turned off the deserted

highroad into the concrete road that ran between tobacco fields to the tire factory. As we left the main road, the woman next to me, Mrs. Kaquini, started to shake uncontrollably. I asked her if she was OK.

"It's the tire factory, Drita," she wailed, pointing toward a large concrete building ahead of us. "My sister says it's been turned into one of those concentration camps. No one who goes in ever comes out alive."

Nineteen

The Factory

About four hundred feet from the factory, we halted before a roadblock manned by several guards in Serb police uniforms. A man in a peaked officer's cap with a rifle slung over his shoulder stepped forward and questioned the driver of the leading jeep. After a brief conversation, he returned to an open shelter beside the road and picked up the telephone.

While the officer was talking, the driver of the jeep said something to the machine gunner sitting beside him. The man grinned, climbed into the back of the vehicle, and swung his weapon around so that it was pointing straight at us.

Mrs. Kaquini grabbed my arm and screamed. "This is it, Drita," she cried. "God have mercy on us!"

The noise disturbed the officer on the telephone. Putting his hand over the mouthpiece, he shouted to the gunner, "Don't be an idiot, man! Can't you see they've had enough?" The gunner laughed and muttered something about it being only a joke. Nevertheless, he lowered his weapon and returned to his seat.

After he had finished his call, the officer went back to the gang. A few more police and a man from the rear jeep sauntered up to see what was going on. They talked for a while, then the officer told one of his men to raise the barrier. The tractors started up and, with a policeman now in the back of each jeep, we passed through the roadblock and continued toward the factory. As we passed, the officer smiled at us and saluted.

The factory, although no longer working, was not a prison camp. The tractors halted near a low building on the left of the parking lot. It was just possible to read the word "canteen" on a peeling sign above the entrance. To our astonishment, one of the policemen unlocked the door and said we were free to use whatever facilities were still working. We swarmed off the wagons and filed inside.

The canteen had clearly not been used for weeks. The smell of old fat hung in the air and the surfaces were covered with dust. Nevertheless, there was still water in the taps and toilets, and before long the place was filled with the excited chatter of women and children.

After helping Mother with the children, I checked on Grandma before going over to the door where one of the policemen was standing guard. "Could you tell me what's happening, please?" I asked.

The man pushed his cap off his forehead and sighed. "Another messup! God knows who told you all to come down here. You weren't supposed to."

My heart jumped. I knew who had brought the orders for our removal from the village. Was it possible that Zoran had deliberately gotten the orders wrong? "Do you know what's going on up there, in Toskik?" I asked.

The policeman gazed earnestly at me. Looking into his sad, fatherly eyes, I realized he was a family man, perhaps with a daughter my age back home in Serbia. I hoped his wife and children had found somewhere to shelter from the NATO air strikes. "Listen, Miss," he said eventually, "don't blame me. Orders are to clear the villages, that's all. What these thugs get up to is none of my business. There's nothing I can do about it."

I wanted to shout at him, to tell him that it *was* his business, that people like him *could* do something if enough of them cared. But there was no point. The world is not changed by hysterical teenagers. I thanked him for talking to me and went back to join the others.

After we had been at the canteen for about an hour, we were ordered back on the wagons. The policemen helped us aboard, telling us we were being sent back to the village, then climbed into the jeeps. The Thunder, who had not come near the canteen while we were inside, didn't say a word to them.

The police escort left us at the checkpoint. It was now almost midday and the air was thick with dust and fumes from the tractor's exhaust. The children slept. The rest of us talked quietly or sat staring anxiously ahead, fearful of what we would find when we arrived.

Twenty

An Ethnic Cleansing

I don't know who saw the smoke first. All I remember was Mrs. Kaquini pointing to the dark pall hanging over the hillside and saying, "Oh, dear! The Gecis' compound is still alight."

I didn't tell her, but I knew she wasn't right. The Gecis' fire had almost burned out when we left. Besides, the dense, billowing clouds that rose above Toskik could not have been the result of a single blaze.

The men in the leading jeep saw the smoke, too. They pointed it out to us with cruel, obscene gestures. When we reached the turning for the village, the jeeps remained on the main road while the tractors turned off and stopped just below the bridge. The drivers then set the tractors alight before running back to their colleagues. As soon as they were on board, the vehicles turned and sped off towards Pec, horns blaring.

Some of the villagers, desperate to find out what had

happened to their homes and menfolk, set off up the lane right away. The others, ourselves included, chose to rest by the river and work out what to do. As there was plenty of daylight left, Mother and I decided to walk up to the village alone. Grandma agreed to stay behind with the children until we returned with whatever food we could find.

"Why can't we all come, Mama?" complained Rukie. "I want to go home."

"We all want to go home, Rukie, darling," replied Mother, who was now back in control of herself. "But first Drita and I must check that those horrible men have gone."

Her explanation was only partly true, of course. The main reason why we didn't want the children with us was to save them from whatever horrors we might find. It proved a wise decision.

Long afterward we learned that the Thunder had hung around the village for about an hour after we had gone, waiting for orders. Finally, losing patience, the gang had gone on an orgy of murder and destruction before driving away. About twenty of the men we had left behind had managed to escape by rushing one of the trucks and fleeing into the fields. The rest – fifteen fathers, brothers, sons – had been shot and their bodies burned.

There was no plan to the devastation. Some houses, including the Sakics', were untouched. Others had been sprayed with machine-gun bullets, blown apart with grenades, or set on fire. I counted twenty-one that were still burning.

Too shocked to speak, Mother and I made our way slowly through what remained of our community. At the crossroad we saw bloodstains on the ground and long marks in the dust where the bodies had been dragged away. Passing on, we came to the road where we had lived. Of the nine houses, only three were still standing.

All that remained of our home were blackened stone walls. The interior had been gutted by fire. Amid the ashes lay the charred skeletons of all we had possessed – furniture, household goods, clothes, bedding, and toys. Everything had been destroyed. The gang had even burned the shed where Father had kept his garden tools.

For several minutes we stood staring at the smoldering ruins of our life. Eventually, perhaps hoping to find something that had escaped the blaze, we walked around to the back of the house. It was no different, just scorched stones and ugly dark holes where the door and windows had been.

Although the fire had burned an uneven brown fringe around the walls, most of the grass in the backyard was untouched. Walking across to the bushes, I found the mark made by Father's shot. Bittersweet memories flooded my mind.

I glanced across to where the washline had hung. One of the poles had been snapped off at ground level. The other leaned to one side, trailing the broken line. Near the top, held by a single peg, was a small cream envelope. I took it down with shaking hands.

It was addressed in bold letters to Drita Binaku. Underneath, the sender had added hastily in pencil: "*I am so sorry. I did what I could and I hope you are all safe. After the war I will explain. Always, Zoran.*"

Inside the envelope, wrapped in a sheet of soft tissue paper, was my watch.

Twenty-one

Uncollected Mail

*M*y dear Zoran,

I've often tried to write this letter, but each time I've ripped it up because it didn't sound right. I hope this one turns out OK.

I'd better say right away that we all now know the truth – and you're a bit of hero in these parts! You made up those orders about the women and children being wanted at the tire factory, didn't you? You were trying to save us. But at the time, when I saw you wearing that blacking and talking to your uncle . . . well, if someone had given me a gun, I think I'd have shot you! Sorry. I should have trusted you and realized what was going on.

Of course, we'll never know what you saved us from. Perhaps not even the Thunder would have killed women and children. But there was no way of telling, and you knew better than anyone what they were capable of.

Did you see what they did? I hope not, but since you left my watch (how did you do it?) you must know something, so I won't describe it. But I think you ought to know that Grandpa and Mr. Halili were both killed.

After we had seen what the Thunder had done, we were so terrified of the gang returning that we ran away into the woods. Father and the other men from the village who'd escaped soon found us. Some families fled to Albania. The rest of us stayed in hiding, living like fugitives. If living rough sounds romantic, I promise you it isn't. When we came out, unwashed, starving, and covered in sores, people said they could smell us a mile away.

The British were the first NATO forces to reach Toskik. Their tanks and armored cars rolled in one Sunday afternoon, all neat and tidy and professional-looking. Such a contrast to the KLA and the Thunder! The soldiers were very kind and put up tents and other shelters for the homeless, including ourselves.

Then came the aid workers and journalists. Because of the massacre, lots of investigators came to Toskik, all trying to find out what had happened. We talked to them quite freely at first, but after a while all we wanted was to be left in peace to rebuild our lives. As you said when we first met, the past is Kosovo's problem – we must try to forget it.

I made friends with a reporter named Anna from an

American newspaper. When I told her our story, she promised to try and discover what had happened to you. All she learned was that you'd been seen riding away from Pec on the afternoon of the massacre. As she spoke only English, I'm surprised she managed to find out even that. In the end, her paper recalled her to cover another story. They said Kosovo was yesterday's news.

So where did you get to, Zoran? And, more important, where are you now? Please, if you receive this letter, get in touch and tell me that you're safe. Even Father wants to know – he calls you his "young Serb ally!"

Toskik is gradually getting back to normal, although no Serbs live here now. The whole family has recovered well. I'm back at school and Father has started up his business again. Without Uncle Ali's help, however, he doesn't make much money. Remember my nice sneakers? I still wear them, even though they're worn through at the toes. No new shoes for the Binakus nowadays! All our spare money is spent rebuilding our house, which should be finished before the winter.

I'm getting boring, aren't I? What I really want to say is that I miss you so very much. I'm going to put this letter in our mailbox (it's still there!), just in case you happen to be passing . . .

With all my love (which is a lot),
Drita

The next afternoon I dropped my letter into the milk can. Every day, on the way back from school, I check to see if it's still there. It is. Last week, during a heavy storm, rain got into the can. The letter now lies in a puddle of rusty water – in another couple of weeks it'll probably have rotted away completely.

I'm not sure I can bring myself to write another.

Historical Notes

On June 10, 1999, NATO and Serb commanders signed a peace agreement by which the Serbs agreed to withdraw all armed forces, including police, from Kosovo. NATO then provided the core of the 46,000-strong multinational Kosovo Force (KFOR), which entered the province to restore law and order. Under its cover, some 1.3 million Kosovo Albanian refugees returned home. Thousands of civilian Kosovo Serbs had already fled to Serbia. Those who remained needed the constant protection of KFOR soldiers.

We do not know how many Kosovo Albanians were killed in the ethnic cleansing. After the discovery of several mass graves, initial estimates were as high as 100,000. Later, this figure was reduced to 2,000–3,000. Steps were taken to arrest and put on trial those guilty of ordering and carrying out the horrific mass murders.

A year after the end of the war, the situation in Kosovo

remained extremely difficult. President Milosevic was still in power, refusing to surrender Serbia's claim to Kosovo. Racial tension in the province itself remained high and its economy and government relied heavily on the continued presence of KFOR. There was little hope that Drita and Zoran's dream of a peaceful, multiethnic Kosovo would become reality for many years.

President Milosevic finally fell from power in October 2000. His successor, Vojislav Kostunica, a Serb nationalist, offered no immediate solution to the problem of Kosovo.

Further Information

If you would like to find out more about Kosovo, these books will help:

Malcolm, Noel. *Kosovo – A Short History* (Macmillan, London, 1996).

Ross, Stewart. *The War in Kosovo* (Hodder Wayland, London, 2000).

Different viewpoints on the Kosovo crisis can be found on these web sites:

Serb: http://www.gov.yu

Kosovo Albanian: http://www.kosovapress.com

NATO: http://nato.int

Glossary

Air strikes Attacks on land targets by military aircraft.

Artillery Large guns used in warfare on land.

Balkans The lands to the east of the Adriatic Sea, populated by a wide range of racial and religious groups.

Compound A group of houses belonging to members of the same extended family and usually enclosed by a wall.

Ethnic Cleansing The process by which the Serbs tried to alter the racial balance in Kosovo (and other regions in the area) by getting rid of non-Serbs. It involved the destruction of homes, forced emigration, and, on occasion, mass murder.

Guerrillas Irregular soldiers who fight by hit-and-run raids and ambushes rather than pitched battles.

Human Rights Watch An independent group that researches breaches of human rights worldwide.

Kalashnikov A popular Russian-made machine gun.

KLA The Kosovo Liberation Army, a radical pro-Albanian force dedicated to driving the Serbs from Kosovo.

Massacre The slaughter of a large group of people.

Milosevic Slobodan Milosevic, the leader of Serbia from 1987–2000.

NATO The North Atlantic Treaty Organization, a military alliance set up in 1949 to defend the West against communist Russia.

Orthodox The eastern branch of the Christian Church, originally based in Constantinople (Istanbul). It had branches throughout Russia, eastern Europe, and the Middle East.

Province A large region or district of a country.

Rugova Ibrahim Rugova, the head of the Democratic League of Kosovo who tried to get greater independence for his country by democratic means.

Thunder, the A made-up name, but similar in style to those used by semiofficial gangs of Serb thugs who practiced the more extreme forms of ethnic cleansing.

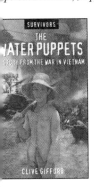

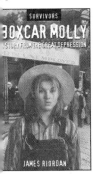
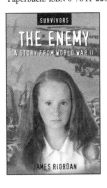